Mafia Camorra and Casal di Principe

Money, Silence and Blood. The true story of the Camorra in Campania

Introduction

This book tells true stories of the Mafia, 'Ndrangheta and Neapolitan Camorra. We will mention places, dates, names and nicknames of the history of the Casalesi Di Casal di Principe in the Casertano, where one of the major Camorra activities in Campania took place after the rise of Raffaele Cutolo (or professor of Vesuviano (4 November 1941 - 17 February 2021)), the boss of the 70s to 90s, where hundreds of crimes between rival clans have been. We will talk about the highest bosses in history such as Francesco Schiavone, Michele Zagaria, Mario Iovine, the Ciro Nuvoletta clan and many other Bosses who made the history of the twentieth century.

After long searches, all the testimonies regarding the Camorra families, the Spartacus trial, we have testimonies of Dario De Simone collaborator with justice and repentant of his past actions in the families of the clans. Testimonies of prosecutors, lawyers and sentences in courtrooms, testimonies of daughters of people murdered for not having paid the protection of the Camorra, who rebelled for their freedom and for not having participated in extortion.

The Camorra at that time also wanted to assassinate the famous writer of the book Gomorrah, Roberto Saviano, who was placed under police escort, and much more, we will find the recorded phone call of the two bosses who force the writer to stop the manuscript before he something bad can happen. We will find quotes from Renato Natale former mayor of Casal di Principe, testimonies of journalists and writer Rosaria Capacchione, and even Lorenzo Diana of the University of Naples Federico II and senator of the Italian Republic, who tells the story of those past times and much more…

I highly recommend to all readers to pay close attention to events and names connected with places and dates to fully understand the story. We will quote names and descriptions in parentheses to move from one testimony to another to connect consecutive dates and events.

I wish you a pleasant journey into the world of our reading.

Casalesi, money, silence and blood

Palermo, which seems to indicate only ugly, very ugly things, monstrous entities that seem to have been carved in history immobile in time, always the same. Instead, once those words indicated people, all different individuals, each with their history and destiny, once for example, if they said Corleonesi, we meant the inhabitants of Corleone province of Palermo, now instead of when we are with the word, we indicate above all one of the most powerful and bloodthirsty groups what our Sicilian mafia.

And so also for the Casalesi, who should only be the inhabitants of Casal di Principe province of Caserta and instead with that Casalesi name, usually one of the richest, powerful and dangerous criminal groups is indicated. Monstrous entities, motionless over time and it does not matter if those who are part of it are sometimes not born in Corleone or Casal di Principe and maybe there has never been any from those countries, but that's the way it is, it's not an invention, the mafia of the province of Caserta the Camorra of the Casalesi exists and to the horrendous meaning we know.

To understand how it happened, we need to start thinking that behind the words there are people, stories of people who, for better or worse, have had to deal with those words, those who gave them the negative meaning and those who fight instead. because you go back to having a clean one.

For example, there is a gentleman named Federico, Federico Del Prete. Mr Federico is in his office via Baracca in the centre of Casal di Principe, it is already late in the evening but it doesn't matter that he always goes late to the office Mr Federico, there is a lot to work for, for those who manage a small union, S.N.A. is called a union Autonomous national ambulant and it is not so small, with 3000 registered all the street vendors in the area, there is a lot to work, but Mr Federico likes to work. It is not an easy job because that is not an easy area, there are the Casalesi in Casal di Principe, but not the inhabitants of the town, the Casalesi like Camorra. Mr Federico is worried, the next day he has to go and testify in a trial against a traffic policeman from Mondragone, a nearby town because he was arrested on charges of being the collector of the local clan's protection money, it is not the first once Mr Federico makes a complaint of this kind, against the protection money and the harassment that street vendors in the squares and markets suffer from the Camorra, Mr Federico is worried and even a little scared but he is not one to hold back that so he will testify tomorrow and in the meantime, he works late as always. He is phoning with the tax accounts of the street vendors in his hand to check when he notices something, there is a man at the door of the office looking at him, stories of people, there is a man named Francesco, Francesco Schiavone and also the nickname that he doesn't like, they call him Sandokan, because of his beard. Sandokan stands motionless, in silence, and with him, other people standstill, a woman a man two small girls motionless and in silence, outside that room beyond a granite wall that runs on a track, that secret refuge hides of 3 rooms with bathroom and kitchen there is the rest of the villa in via Salerno near the centre of Casal di Principe. But there are also other men 40 armed men in uniform, who have been looking for him for less than 13 hours without finding him, it seems the beginning of a film, it looks like the battle of Algiers by Gillo Pontecorvo, only the man who is hidden behind the wall is not a warrior who fights for the liberation of his people as in the film, on the contrary, those who want to free him, the people, the people are those men in uniform the agents of the DIA the Anti-Mafia Investigative Directorate while instead, the one who the people oppress him the people he is Francesco Schiavone known as Sandokan, one of the leaders of the Casalesi

Camorra who exploits and terrorizes the whole area. And then there is another man, a young man, he is 27 years old, his name is Roberto, Roberto Saviano. He is a writer and has written a book called Gomorrah and which is having great success mainly thanks to the word of mouth of readers. Roberto is on stage, in the main square of Casal di Principe, the Piazza del Mercato, because there is a demonstration for the legality that against the Camorra, a big thing, there is also the president of the Chamber Fausto Bertinotti, all there in the land of the Casalesi Camorra, leaders such as Francesco Schiavone Antonio Iovine and Michele Zagaria. Talking It touches the writer when he talks about the Camorra, but here is what happens to the writers when they feel inside something, they have to say at all costs that they have to tell.

Roberto Schiavone declares: "On stage maybe something happens in me, at least I say, who has more to do with the belly and the head, that is, I feel a little bit with blood in my eyes, but because

I see so many guys, so many guys middle school students, divided by sex, among other things, incredible mask dresses, all there in those areas, in short it was easy to imagine their destiny and then at a certain point I say, that it's raining Zagaria since you don't want anything go away this land does not belong to you, and I tell the guys, say their names, you can do it, now I have been asking for a choice of course, say the name of a boss, not putting them in danger, the nonsense, but the respect of not saying his name in vain that leads him to say that, you saw that he never burned it, never that if he says Zagaria Michele or Schiavone Francesco, in via Corso Umberto, in a farmhouse in the market square where I then pronounced those names what happens to you he makes you punish but not at all, it is respect, it is a kind of code that you pass, and that you grow up with, that it is better to pronounce them a little, their presence is useless to evoke it when there is no need, so I name these names and I say this and immediately I feel the cold ".

The frost, because we are in Casal di Principe, the homeland of the Casalesi, but not the common people, the normal people, the respectable people who live in the village in the Casalesi, the Camorra, the Caserta mafia.

When we say Camorra, Naples and clans immediately come to mind, killing each other in the streets for the control of the city's neighbourhoods, Secondigliano, Scampia, Spanish neighbourhoods, the market square and the lace streets dominated by about forty groups of emerging demons and splinters. in violent and bloody anarchy. Or else it comes to mind Raffaele Cutolo, who in the 80s and 90s extended the authority of his new organized Camorra to almost all of Campania before being defeated by the rival clans by the action of the police and by the revelations of the repentant ones. And those Casalesi, the Camorra of the province of Caserta, which revolves around the towns of Casal di

Principe, San Cipriano and Casapesenna, are another thing, for convenience, we continue to call them Camorra, but they, the Casalesi are mafia. In Campania in the 1970s, two Camorra families are so tied to Cosa Nostra for business reasons that the Sicilian Mafia affiliates them among men of honour. The first is the Michele Zaza Clan, which controls the smuggling of cigarettes arriving at the port of Naples, the other is the Nuvoletta family from Marano near Naples, which controls the province of Caserta. The brothers Lorenzo, Angelo and Ciro Nuvoletta, are known and become men and honour linked first Stefano Bontade and then also the Corleonesi, in their estate a large Masseria Poggio Vallesana near Marano the fugitives of Cosa Nostra are hiding and There are meetings with bosses of the calibre of Bontade, Riina and Pippo Calò. And at Nuvoletta's house, Sicilian fugitives such as Gaspare Mutolo are affiliated with Cosa Nostra. Smuggling cigarettes, extortion, large landholdings with traditional buffalo farms, the

Nuvoletta brothers' control much of the province of Caserta, but in the meantime, something has happened in Naples, Raffaele Cutolo has arrived. The newly-organized Camorra of Raffaele Cutolo wants to extend its hegemony over Naples and the whole countryside, there is a lot of money at stake, especially that of the Reconstruction after the 1980 earthquake. The new family is born, which against Raffaele Cutolo brings together Boss as Carmine Alfieri and Umberto Ammaturo. Also allied to the new family are the Nuvoletta di Marano. War breaks out, 250 deaths a year, which between 1978-1983 caused at least 1500 deaths. Among the men of cloud who fight against Cutolo, there is one, in particular, his name is Antonio Bardellino, the true story of the Casalesi of the mafia in the province of Caserta begins with him.

Antonio Bardellino is also a mafia member, affiliated with Cosa Nostra, they started him in the Masseria of Nuvoletta in the presence of the Cosa Nostra bosses like Saro Riccobono, joined on the finger, Santina to hold in his hands until the words of the oath are completely burned. Important friendships, such as Stefano Bontate, Gaetano Badalamenti and also the boss of the Two Worlds Tommaso Buscetta, Antonio Bardellino has made a career out of it, since he was only a robber of San Cipriano who stopped on the street, now after the progressive defeat of Raffaele Cutolo of his new organized Camorra who retires from the province, who decides together Nuvoletta and him Bardellino.

Bardellino, has had an extraordinary role in the history of the crime Camorra because the first Camorra entrepreneur who makes investments in South America, has contact with the big drug traffickers, makes investments in Spain first and even his profile is also a profile let's say very important in the Camorra is an unknown profile until a certain period.

Money, investments, entrepreneurial skills and silence, are the two main elements of our history, the history of the Casalesi, the car of the province of Caserta, a mafia of which no one seems to notice at that moment and even after, even if that mafia, at that moment is also after a lot of noise.

Money and silence, let's remember because we'll talk about it again later, money, silence and blood.

Antonio Bardellino can count on a fire group of a few hundred men, almost all of them from Casal di Principe, Casapesenna and San Cipriano. People like Mario Iovine who robbed trucks with him and who has now become his right hand, like Raffaele Diana, like the brothers Antonio and Paride Salzillo, and then two young men from Casal di Principe Francesco Schiavone known as Sandokan because of the bar and Francesco Bidognetti known as 'Cicciotto at midnight'. Antonio Bardellino is not just a group of young people ready to make good connections with local politics, his brother Ernesto for example becomes mayor of the town of San Cipriano with the Socialist Party, it is not easy to do politics, politics honestly in such a context.

Lorenzo Diana, former parliamentarian as head of the Anti-Mafia observatory declares: "We had perceived that the Camorra is advancing, and advancing with substantial impunity, as the Camorra got their hands on all sectors of social and economic life, it was taking root, becoming a monster and the state not opposed to it, a Casalesi clan and could have become what it is today because it was not opposed in its time, not only was it not opposed but this face was also supported and was also facilitated by some conclusions. "

Antonio Bardellino is the boss of the Casalesi, he has a princely villa San Cipriano, but there is not much left because he always travels, South America, Brazil, Spain, first as a self-styled entrepreneur than as a fugitive when it is understood that his criminal depth, one so not he can stay under the others and the others do not trust to be next to him the others, in this case, are the Nuvoletta brothers and their allies' clans such as the Gionta family of Torre Annunziata. In the mafia, there is only one way to resolve fears, conflicts and lack of trust, to kill.

And so, after the one against the newly organized Camorra by Raffaele Cutolo, another war broke out in the province of Caserta.

Interview with Dario De Simone, collaborator of justice declares: "My first murder took place in the summer of '84, immediately after my release from prison, indeed from the OPG of Pozzo di Gotto in the province of Messina, he was an affiliate of the Nuvoletta clan which was a clan against us and took place in an attacked country, adjacent to us and that is it was my first murder ... after that murder, clearly I was sworn in at Casal di Principe. "

Bardellino and Casalesi are the strongest. In June 1984, 14 armed and masked men broke through the gate and broke into the Masseria of Nuvoletta in Poggio Vallesana. In the Masseria there is one of the Nuvoletta Ciro brothers, who tries to escape but chases them to the road, they shoot him in the back like a rifle and then finish him off with a pistol shot. Ciro Nuvoletta is not the only one to die on that day, there is a boy named Salvatore Squillace and at 16, he has nothing to do with the Camorra, and I am a 16-year-old boy who is in passing by chance in those parts but runs into Bardellino's men who come out shooting and is killed by a stray bullet. Then a few months later in August 1984, the Barbellino men dealt the second blow, hidden inside a tourist bus, 15 Barbellino men approached the Circolo of Piscator of Torre Annunziata where there is a baptism, in which many of the Gionta clan.

Bardellino's men jump out with weapons and bulletproof vests and start shooting, 104 Bossoli and 8 dead, plus 7 wounded, remain on the ground, including people who have nothing to do with an 8-year-old girl. A massacre, the massacre in the fishermen's club.

Antonio Bardellino also wins this war, the Nuvoletta clan is forced to step aside, also paying a kind of commitment to Peace.

Luigi Di Fioredi, journalist and writer declare: "Usually it happens this way, in the Mafia groups, in the Camorra groups, one would give one's head to someone dangerous, so either they have them arrested or even killed. One of the neighbours of peace between the Gionta, Nuvoletta and Alfieri, Bardellino was the head of Valentino Gionta. Then a fugitive. Valentino Gionta He was conducting his fugitive in Marano then in the area of Nuvoletta, he was arrested right there after the fugitive."

Another journalist from the Morning, whose name is Giancarlo Siani, Siani is good. He is the one who loves his work and does it with passion, he writes about what happens in Torre Annunziata, uncomfortable but true articles, which talk about relationships between politics and organized crime. Giancarlo Siani is good, he knows how to read well what is happening on his part, even too much for someone.

Luigi Di Fiore comments: Giancarlo Siani wrote a historical article, also from judicial sources at the time and hypothesizes one of the investigative ways on this arrest, that is, he said that it could be the arrest of Gionta, the price that had been paid for the peace with Bardellino and with Alfieri by the Nuvoletta group and therefore in exchange he had had Gionta arrested on his territory perhaps with a tip-off, writing this, Giancarlo Siani had practically given the infamous to Lorenzo Nuvoletta, there was a meeting in the Masseria di Marano and it was decided the murder of Giancarlo Siani.

October 23, 1985, 9:00 pm. Giancarlo Siani is parking his little Mehari under his house at Vomero, when two men who have been waiting for him undisturbed for some time approach, take out their guns and shoot him. Giancarlo Siani is not the only innocent victim of those times of war, before there was a Carabiniere from Marano called Salvatore Nuvoletta, he has nothing to do with the Nuvoletta clan and a very common surname in those parts, Salvatore is only a 20-year-old Carabiniere that day. That day is July 2,

1982, he stands in front of his parents' shop playing with a child, then suddenly Salvatore hears himself called out loud by name and surname, he has nothing to do with the Camorra Salvatore but he is anyway from those parts and he is a Carabiniere and knows what can happen when someone calls you that, he just has time to push the child away, when two men unload a 357 Magnum loaded with explosive bullets on him twice. Why? Why did they kill him like that? There was a firefight a short time before with the Carabinieri and Mario Schiavone is known as Menelik, Sandokan's cousin was killed. The Casalesi want the head of those who killed Menelik, if this Salvatore Nuvoletta, this carabiniere who has nothing to do with it because, among other things, when there was a firefight he was also off duty, but he is the youngest and the less protected, then someone makes his name and Salvatore is killed.

Luigi Di Fiore declares: "The Casale does not make a species they do not have problems killing to give warnings in a transversal way one of the illustrious victims is the brother of judge Imposimato in the early 80s, who was a favour done to the Sicilian Mafia. to give a warning to the judge who was investigating in Rome precisely on the relationship between the Banda della Magliana and the Sicilian Mafia. "

And then there are the men of the police forces, such as the Carabinieri Carmelo Ganci and Luciano Pignatelli, and also 10 prison police officers on duty at the prisons of Poggioreale and Santa Maria Capua Vetere, like Ignazio De Florio, who was killed on the same day by Franco Imposimato.

Eventually, Antonio Bardellino and his men find themselves masters of the province of Caserta, masters of what has begun to be the empire of the Casalesi. An empire in full expansion, especially from an economic point of view.

Federico Cafiero of the prosecutor of the Spartacus trial declares: "Antonio Bardellino was a man who had a large following of great economic intelligence and it was with his management that the organization began to prosper by infiltrating public procurement by controlling the municipalities and controlling the concrete market, that of quarries, that of aggregates, was a real economic explosion that the organization had in the period in which Bardellino led it.

There is a lot of money at stake, there are many works to be done in the province of Caserta, useful works that serve the development of the territory, especially after the 1980 earthquake.

There is the highway that goes from Nola to Villa Literno to put okay, there is the connection of the Rome-Naples motorway to be built, there are public tenders for almost 250 billion lire, we are starting to talk about high speed, and then there is a huge job the arrangement of the 320 km of the banks of the Regi Lagni canal in reclamation work that dates back to the time of the Bourbons, a deal worth almost 500 billion of the old lire. Thanks to the control of the territory, direct intimidation, corruption and relations with politics, Antonio Bardellino and his team get their hands everywhere. They make money in two ways, asking for protection money from the companies that do the work, 10% for contracts concerning the roads and 5% for those concerning the edition, but above all, if they take the contracts, because when you build something you need a series of companies that work on-site for earthmoving digging with bulldozers for example, or for building materials such as concrete, which must be done on-site because you have to use it and between a couple of hours.

Maurizio Vallone, deputy chief executive officer of the Naples DIA states: "They then created three consortia, 1 for cement, 1 for aggregates, 1 for other materials, other building materials in which all the entrepreneurs who wanted to operate in this sector had to join in fact and to this consortium, those who did not join were forced to either exit the market or were physically eliminated. "

Clean companies, those that have the Anti-Mafia certification in a place like that of the north, for example, win the contracts, but then they are forced to subcontract to the Casalesi companies, at the price they want, of course, that's what happens for example, for the contract from the prison of Santa Maria Capua Vetere which is won by a large oil company, specialized in public construction.

Raffaele Magi, Director Regulator of the Spartacus process declares: "The contract for the prison is won by a large company in Parma, as soon as the manager of the Parma company arrives on site, not only is he slapped by people belonging to the organization, because he does not understand immediately with whom he is talking, but the following evening he is put in the car, let's say he is driven around the countryside of Agro Aversano and is brought in front of Francesco Bidognetti and is told, with a certain amount of amazement, and not only comes inside him who has to provide all the materials, let's say for the completion of the prison, the iron, the doors, the bathrooms, I would like to say the keys. "

To do this, however, to decide who, how and how much work in the province of Caserta, we need a capillary control of the territory, we need people who know immediately as soon as a construction site is opened somewhere and even just a municipality, an administration wants to launch a contract and above all be able to control it. In short, it takes mayors, counsellors and administrators, complacent or colluding for love or force.

Lorenzo Diana, Former Parliamentary DS of the Anti-Mafia Observatory declares: "In a short time, the Camorra begins to decide not only by whom to be represented but begins to impose mayors, councillors, administrators in health companies, in 1979 there is the first formation of a supported civic list was wanted by Iovine in Casal di Principe. "

Complacent administrators, complacent bank managers, able to receive rivers of money without asking questions and then companies and businesses to launder it, white-collar workers not just soldiers who can shoot, but entrepreneurs who can make money.

Lorenzo Diana declares: "We were weak because there was no awareness in the population who had a delay in the perception of the presence of the Camorra in a capillary way, we often felt objected, but who interests us, there is a part of criminal activities such as in many other parts of Italy and the world, but something original, more alarming, was coming to them. "

Antonio Bardellino is at the top of the various clans that rule the Casalesi empire, but there are also others, those who know how to shoot, those who struggle to respect his authority as he did not respect that of Nuvoletta, there are these young people that are growing. There is Francesco Bidognetti, there is Francesco Schiavone Sandokan, there is another young man who is growing up, Michele Zagaria, there is Enzo De Falco known as 'Il Lupo', and there is also Bardellino's right arm, Mario Iovine.

There is one thing that does not add up though, Antonio Bardellino makes a lot of money with the Casalesi companies or with his own, but then takes them out abroad, to South America, to Brazil, to invest in drug trafficking. And in fact, it is the one who lives abroad, delegates everything to his brothers and nephews and you live in Brazil and not in its territory and this is something that no head of either the Cosa Nostra or the Camorra has ever done. A boss feels certain things, and Antonio Bardellino did not become the leader of the Casalesi so by chance, then, towards the end of 1987 I leave Brazil to return to San Cipriano, he has to fix a few things, which means a very specific thing, to kill a few people.

Mario Iovine, Bardellino's right arm to a brother named Domenico, does not behave well with Domenico, now and then He talks to the Carabinieri. So, one day in January 1988 at 10 in the morning, the car with Domenico Iovino and his bodyguard on board is flanked along the Domiziana state road by a car carrying a small group of Casalesi, who begin to shoot, Domenico Iovine is killed with 5 shots loaded with buckshot, it is a signal, a signal given to Mario Iovine and all the other Guaglioni of the Casalesi family, it is they who are not there.

Dario De Simone, Repentant and collaborator of justice says: "At that point, it was decided to kill Bardellino Antonio, here we are talking about '88, I was aware of it every day, also because I was under house arrest, but all every day I would leave the house quietly because the controls were not there ... and I met with De Falco, clearly we were aware of what was to happen."

Antonio Bardellino is back in Brazil and it is there that Mario Iovine contacts him, Antonio Bardellino does not trust him, and so on May 26, 1988, he gives him an appointment in Buzios which is about a hundred kilometres from Rio de Janeiro and awaits him there...

Dario De Simone continues to tell: "... We were waiting for the news that Iovine Mario would call from Brazil to tell them all right, Tonino is dead, you can go ahead and kill the grandchildren."

The death of Antonio Bardellino remains a mystery, according to the statements of the repentance it was Mario Iovine who killed him with a hammer after Bardellino had found the gun he had hidden in the house to shoot. Then Iovine had buried him on a beach in a place that was never found, but for someone else, Antonio Bardellino would still be alive, he agreed with Iovine and the Casalesi and then withdrew. Whatever happened, Mario Iovine's phone call to the men who are waiting in Casal di Principe arrives, and another slaughter begins.

Raffaele Magi councillor says: "From there a chain of blood is born that lasts a couple of years and that has episodes of extraordinary military violence, to think that in December 1988 in front of a gambling den in Casapesenna in a firefight between people trust Barbellino who was trying to resist the offensive and the people who are currently the managers, let's say of the current great Casalesi, something like 140 to 150 shots of automatic weapons is exploded, double those that were found on the pavement of the street, In short, just to understand. "

Attention, silence again, episodes that would bring reporters from all over the world, and which instead end up in the news pages of the local Editions, and instead in Casal di Principe throughout the province of Caserta there is war.

The Casalesi act quickly, the first to be killed and Paride Salzillo, one of Antonio Bardellino's nephews, without knowing what happened, Antonio Bardellino in Brazil, Paride Salzillo goes on a date, finds himself in front of Francesco Schiavone Sandokan his men take away his gun, they tell him that Bardellino is dead and that now it's his turn, so Salzillo sits down on a chair and lets himself be strangled practically without reacting.

Again, Dario says: "... perhaps later, to destroy the whole family of Bardellino, I did the murders within the group of Bardellino, of his nephew Antonio who was now detached from the group of Casalesi, and then there was "the so-called Casapesenna massacre, where ... we had an infiltrator within the group of Salzillo Antonio who was the nephew of Bardellino, and this ambush was organized"

To the men of Antonio Salzillo, the other nephew of Bardellino, the only able to organize a reaction, a tip arrived: Raffaele Diana, one of Sandokan's men, is playing in a Bisca in Casapesenna.

It is a trap, Raffaele Diana acts only as bait, and so when Antonio Salzillo arrives with his men there are also those of the others and a firefight breaks out. Antonio Salzillo is saved and escapes to Switzerland, but that evening, on the evening of 17 December 1988 in Casapesenna there is the far west, and not only there, in San Cipriano and Casal di Principe, an armed procession in cars parades along with the courses of the towns, there under the house of Bardellino.

Lorenzo Diana declares: "It is the clear sign of an almost South American transformation of those territories in which the Camorra could act undisturbed to the point of transmitting an armed procession. "

The war ends with the escape of the last family of Antonio Bardellino. The Camorra of the province of Caserta passes into the hands of Mario Iorio, who heads a sort of directorate made up of Sandokan, Francesco Bidognetti and Enzo De Falco, but Mario Iovine does not have the authority to keep them all under control, he is not Antonio Bardellino. Indeed, he has a lot of problems too, in the meantime he has a problem with cocaine and then like Bardellino makes the mistake of moving all his business abroad, no, the authority to keep everyone under control, Mario Iovine just doesn't have it. It has. Sandokan and Francesco Bidognetti are in prison, they are arrested by the Carabinieri thanks to a tip while they were meeting in the house of the former deputy mayor and finance councillor of Casal di Principe, but it does not matter, they also command from prison without a problem and decide Enzo De Falco it is not reliable and must be eliminated. Maybe it was he who tipped off the Carabinieri who made them end up inside. It would not be the first time that certain things have happened in the Camorra we have already seen.

Raffaele Cantone, Magistrate declares: "De Falco was in some way the entrepreneur in the club, the man of reference and this worried Schiavone and Bidognetti about the fact that I could use a whole series of relationships to the detriment of the other two friends. . "

In February 1991, around 7 pm, Enzo De Falco is in his car in Casal di Principe, at Corso Garibaldi he is flanked by another car with two Casalesi killers on board, Enzo De Falco is hit from a barrage of Kalashnikov and dies instantly. It is the beginning of a new war, De Falco's brother,

Nunzio, tries to react and takes it out on Mario Iovine who is staying in Portugal and has not held back the others, hires a group of Spanish killers who they are not surprised in Cascais Where he lives in a telephone booth while he is phoning and they kill him in March 1991. It is war, the men of De Falco on one side and those of Sandokan dei Bidognetti on the other fight almost every day between Casapesenna, Casal di Principe and San Cipriano, leaving dozens of dead on the ground and not just Camorra soldiers. On March 19, 1995, it is 7.30 in the morning, and Don Peppino is in the Sacristy, preparing for mass, shortly before he celebrated his name day together with a group of friends, many friends because if the Camorra wants him badly, there are many people who instead of loving them for their commitment and courage. He wrote an appeal against what he calls the armed dictatorship of the Camorra which is called for the love of my people. That morning of March 19 just outside the sacristy, Don Peppino finds himself in front of a man, he is a killer Di Nunzio De Falco, he has a semi-automatic Browning in his hand and points at Don Peppino and shoots him 4 shots in the head. When this happens, when someone is killed who is fighting against the armed dictatorship of the spots in Calabria, Sicily or Campania, whether he is a statesman or a respectable citizen, the same thing always happens. There is the pain of respectable people there is the state that is dismayed, indignant and committed as in the song Don Raffaè, by Fabrizio De André, and then inevitably begins the defamation campaign to belittle those who have just been killed. But that's not true, and those who publish certain lies become in one way or another the instrument of that armed dictatorship that was killed by Peppino, who was killed because he was annoying and perhaps also for another, much more subtle, reason.

Federico Cafiero, public prosecutor declares: "However, it was chosen as a target, and I believe this demonstrates what the strategy of the

Casalesi organization is, not so much for the homilies he did, but rather because by killing a man like Don Giuseppe Diana, it would be recalled by the intervention of the State and this would have hindered the evolution and development of illicit trafficking and infiltrations into the legal economy of the Casalesi. And basically, it ended up being the instrument through which the De Falco took their revenge against the Schiavone. "

In the end, the war, Sandokan and Bidognetti win, they kill Giuseppe De Falco brother of Nunzio, they kill the lawyer Aldo Scalzone and De Falco's political adviser, they kill the main killer of the family, they also kill Liano Diana and only the boyfriend of a daughter of the De Falco family, Nunzio De Falco eventually escapes to Spain and retires from business.

At the head of the Camorra in the province of Caserta, at the head of the Casalesi, remain Francesco Bidognetti, known as Cicciotto at midnight, and above all Francesco Schiavone, known as Sandokan. And under them Michele Zagaria called 'Capastorta', Antonio Iovine called 'o` Ninno' and then Dario De Simone, together they rule what is a family federation, the very different Casalesi mafia and we have seen it, from the Neapolitan Camorra.

Rosaria Capacchione, Journalist and writer declares: "To understand how the Casalesi clan works, one must have as a reference, not the Camorra of Scampia, noisy, noisy and very violent, but the Cosa Nostra. Cosa Nostra which over the years has placed its self-protection focus on two fundamental aspects, that of process control and that of concealing the proceeds of illegal activities that took place, money laundering, investments in apparently clean activities, transfers of money abroad, to be able to protect the very survival of organizations regardless of individuals, the Casalesi clan has moved along the same path. "

Before, during and after the war, the Casalesi clan continues to take care of its business, continues to make money, not only with illegal activities, with extortion on contracts and the management of directly controlled companies, not only with concrete and cement. The Casalesi make money with agriculture but not with normal agriculture, not with the products of the earth, fertile land is as rich as Campania. The Casalesi make their money with phantom agriculture. There is a state-called owned company AIMA that collects surplus agricultural products, paying with public money to support agriculture, tons of non-products arrive every year at the AIMA collection centres controlled by the Casalesi. sold, but it's not true, it's rotten fruit, or it's loaded with stones, or it's just a number written on a piece of paper that doesn't match anything. A deal worth hundreds of millions of old lire for each collection point. The Casalesi make money by distributing the products they control almost entirely in bars, restaurants, hotels, canteens, they can only buy and use the products they want, the buffalo mozzarella produced by the Casalesi farms, for example, even those that graze on illegal landfills or those that fall ill with Brucellosis that should be killed, instead, animals that come from the estates of the clans in Romania are killed in their place. The Casalesi make money, they transform everything they touch into gold, even the garbage, even the waste, especially the toxic ones.

Dario confesses: "The Casalesi clan, for someone who does not know, entered the waste business between 1989 and 1990, at that time we knew, understood, the entrepreneurs made us understand the business we didn't know anything about garbage before that day, we didn't know that you could make a lot of money with garbage. "

There is solid urban waste, the abnormal garbage of all the cities of Italy, but above all, there are the poisons that the factories in the North produce, special waste, hospital waste, toxic waste, and those contaminated by radioactive substances.

Rosaria Capacchione declares: "At a certain point, the Camorra that manages to independently manage what was in service up to that moment, done jointly, places itself on the market autonomously above all for the disposal of toxic waste, which is highly industrial waste. dangerous even radioactive. "

But the first to understand the deal is Francesco Bidognetti, Cicciotto is midnight, he puts together a disposal consortium called 'Ecologia 89', closely followed by the others Michele Zagaria and Antonio Iovine, together with entrepreneurs, managers of landfills such as Gaetano Vassallo, are busy to get the garbage of the industries of the North.

Dario De Simone declares: "The waste that came to us mainly came from the north, they came from the Tuscan purifiers, Brescia, they were industrial paint factories, they were industrial laundries, tanneries, everything arrived, I have been many times in landfills, it was hallucinating stuff ... there are some 400/500 meters deep sand pits on the Litorale Domizio, between Castelvolturno and also Cancello Arnone ... in short, everything was unloaded there, everything and more, even to the farmers they told him that it was fertilizer, instead that was boiling, it was mud from the products, everything burned sowing in that area, nothing grows anymore, there is a stench that you can't stay in. "

It is a big deal for companies in the North, disposing of a kg of special waste will cost 2006 prices from 21 to € 0.60 per kilo, the Casalesi do the same for 9 € 0.10 per kilo it is a big deal, it is a criminal business, there is so much money at stake that at a certain point Antonio Iovine comes to mind to ask for the protection money from the companies that dispose of the waste, but it is they, the Casalesi, those companies, and he is pointed out that the Camorra on the Camorra cannot be done.

At first, the waste is secretly buried in official landfills, but it is understood that soon they will get stuck and then someone will find out what is going on. Then illegal landfills are opened in the area between Parete and Villa Literno, the fields are dug, the ditches are filled, the open quarries are used for work, even the roads are used to cover tons of waste. After all, the Casalesi have almost total control of the territory and behave as if it were them. It is as if they could do what they want of 2639 square kilometres of the province of Caserta also poison them, and not just the land, since 1989 since the Casalesi began to massively poison the territory, in the province of Caserta, the number of people who die from cancer linked to pollution increases in an incredible way. Because this is what the mafias do, Cosa Nostra, 'Ndrangheta and the Camorra, even the Casalesi, do not produce work, they steal it from others with rigged contracts, they steal people's money with the inflated costs of public works, they ruin the reputation of those who cultivate the land well and produce excellent buffalo milk, they poison everything with toxic waste because they are entrepreneurs, yes, but criminal entrepreneurs and their task are to make money at all costs. A presence in the area also testified by a display of wealth and power as for the villas of the chiefs, huge, luxurious, Hollywoodian, such as the villa of Walter Schiavone, almost destroyed shortly before a 5 billion-dollar villa was seized by the authorities. lire, 3 floors of neoclassical columns, black marble floors, swimming pools, a bit like the home of Tony Montana the boss in Scarface played by Al Pacino. Because everything that the Casalesi do is not possible without a capillary and almost total control of the territory.

Dario De Simone declares: "The villages in that area and in that area are monitored minute by minute, meter by meter more than the police because everyone brings you news and you know everything about everyone, you can't move, if you tomorrow morning, I give an example, a person buys 30 hectares of land, we know it, it happened! I say this as a personal experience, I went to call an entrepreneur and I said: did you buy 100 hectares of land? He told me how do you know? Nobody knows, only me, the notary and the owner know it! It is so. It is like an entrepreneur with us in the 70s they put bombs to make people pay, after the 70s it was now an absurd fact, a principle is already taken for granted, that every entrepreneur who arrived, before putting the excavator on the ground, was to settle down, he says: I have to do this job, how much does it cost me? This. A fine place. This is the danger of a mafia clan, when you shoot it means that there is some difficulty, when people bring you money without threats, neither with guns nor with words, it means that a principle has been assumed. and therefore, everything is rotten, like a lake of waste when the more you move it the more it stinks."

Control of the territory, which also necessarily means a very close relationship with politics, especially the local one and this is also one thing that makes the difference between the Casalesi mafia of the Neapolitan Camorra.

Raffaele Cantone Magistrate says: "The Casalesi clan has always been very attentive to what was happening in politics, it is no coincidence who Bardellino's brother was for many years, even he personally, mayor, and that is this episode that is told of a possible candidacy for the Senate which was stopped by the leaders of the time, the Socialist Party".

Members of the Casalesi clan families become mayors, councillors and members of the Municipal Councils. There are meetings of clan leaders that are held in the homes of local politicians, such as Gaetano Corvino, deputy mayor of Casal di Principe who is discovered by the police to host Sandokan and Francesco Bidognetti. There are seats manned by clan soldiers on election days, politics is used to obtain contracts, always to make tricks with waste, to avoid checks on construction sites and in landfills.

Dario confesses: "Underworld organizations like ours or any other organization have no reason to exist if these organizations have no ramifications in the social, political, entrepreneurial, law enforcement fabric. They were our entrepreneurs, politicians... local, who then spoke with the politicians who were from the central state. If you don't have these hooks, you have no reason to exist, I can shoot. We don't care so much about politics. We are interested in the works. We were interested in politicians who managed to bring jobs to our area, to demand money ... well ... politics ... it's clear ... and then there was no administration in the province of Caserta, there is no administration where there is no there is infiltration, I challenge anyone, to say that there is no infiltration there, not even the last town in the province of Caserta, there is everywhere because it is so".

Already in 1995 the municipalities dissolved for mafia infiltration in the province of Caserta were 14 which will reach 22 in 2006 more than a third of the administrations in the Caserta area. Some, such as Casal di Principe, dissolved up to 4 times with continuous changes of prefectural commissioners, new elections and new dissolution. But be careful, because there are not only them, the words, as we have said, mean many things and the word Casalesi does not only indicate the Casalesi, the mafia clans of the province of Caserta and does not even indicate only those people in the area who have decided to live with the mafia out of fear or for gain, the consent, the control of the territory, the mafias, both in the province of Caserta and all over the world, obtain it by shooting.

Isaia Sales - Historian says: "In the Casali area, therefore in the Casalesi area, there is the highest number of deaths killed among municipal councillors, councillors, mayors and even municipal officials, which means that the aggression on these local authorities is very strong, and the control is very strong".

There are those people who oppose it, the police, the representatives of the state of course, but also the Casalesi, the respectable Casalesi, those who risk opposition to the armed dictatorship of the Camorra.

Antonio Cangiano, for example, does not want to have anything to do with the Casalesi, but the deputy mayor of Casapesenna and they want him to facilitate their businesses. Antonio Cangiano, however, is not there, and so one day in October 1988, two men approach and shoot him in the legs, nailing him forever in a wheelchair. Antonio Munoz, on the other hand, of the deputy mayor of Mondragone, the La Torre clan would like to be helped in the construction of a clinic, but he is not there. So, one day in July 1990, 6 men go to pick up the farm which he owns and take him away. His body will only be found 13 years later, with 2 shots to the head. Michele Russo, on the other hand, is a trade unionist of the CGIL who deals with construction workers, when they ask for a bribe from the builders, the Casalesi also provide a service let's call it that, no union activities and no strikes, the unionist who tries is beaten and threatened. At the Mexican

Calcestruzzi, for example, wages are too low and then Michele Russo threatens to organize a strike, so one day in January 1991 someone rings the door, Russo goes to open the door and they shoot him in the legs. Federico Del Prete is also a trade unionist, he directs the trade union of itinerant workers he founded in Casal di Principe and it is not easy, because that is precisely the land of the Casalesi and all the commercial activities, even those of the hawkers in the markets are under their control. control. Federico Del Prete denounced it, he denounced above all those who ask for protection money, and lastly, he denounced the Marshal of the Traffic Police of Mondragone, who is called Mattia Sorrentino, is that one of the tax collectors of the La Torre clan.

They have threatened him several times, they have burned his car, but Federico Del Prete is not there, he is a decent person, he is a trade unionist who cares about his dignity and that of his land, he is a hero without knowing it, a small hero small, as the journalist Rosaria Capacchione defined him in which we will talk shortly, people hear this and begin to follow him, his union reaches up to 3000 members and the demonstration against squatters that he organizes in Naples is a great success. The Casalesi do not like all this. So one day in February 2002 Federico Del Prete is in his office as always, even if it is late, and he is worried because the next day there is the trial of Marshal Sorrentino, and he is afraid as right, they have just burned his car, but it goes on the same as always, he is phoning with the tax bills of the peddlers to check in his hand, when he notices something, there is a man at the office door looking at him. That man is a Casalesi killer who shoots him 5 765 calibre rounds, so Federico Del Prete dies, so a little hero die.

Renato Natale, Former Mayor of Casal di Principe declares: "The Camorra here has not established itself without finding any opposition, it is only because it could boast relationships and power in the economy, politics and institutions at all levels and there are now journalistic investigations by the judiciary that show how powerful they could be, so it was somehow also justified that in the end the citizen would return to silence, return home, or no longer have the strength of mobilization and struggle".

Renato Natale is the new mayor of Casal di Principe. The city council has just been dissolved for mafia infiltration and thus new elections are obtained, this time a mayor of the PDS wins them. When Renato Natale became mayor in 1993, the municipality declared bankruptcy, and the first meeting of the city council is held up because there are no more chairs in the council chamber.

Renato Natale declares: "What was under discussion was a question of principle, a cultural question, who ruled. If an institution, freely elected, democratically elected, or the usual suspects or the usual unknowns, then there was a battle of principle that probably took place at that time in that period. I remember when I went to have coffee at the bar and people who crossed and if anything, quietly told me, go ahead, how it goes, it was an attitude the people who demonstrated the desire of the deep desire to be free".

Mayor Natale his folks try to govern according to the public will and the laws, and not according to the will of criminals, they try to do in Casal di Principe what they would do in any other normal country, but it is a continuous war, as the war of the stakes. The municipality decides that the centre of Casal di Principe is a pedestrian area and so it closes it with concrete poles with a chain, this to the Casalesi, the inhabitants of Casal di Principe, that's okay, however, it's not good for the Casalesi, the mafia of Casal di Principe, who every Saturday pull up the stakes and bring them in front of the mayor's house, who takes them back to the square, seems ridiculous, but it is not true, it is a matter of principle of control of the territory and in this, the mayor Natale bother.

Renato Natale says: "Some time ago I had the opportunity to read in the newspaper a statement from a repentant of the Camorra who stated that they had planned in the period in which they were syndrome in Casal di Principe in '94, the Camorra had been planned for my elimination physics, he had to open an accident for which they were looking for an Albanian who had to pretend to be drunk, take advantage of the fact that I used to ride a bicycle he would put me under the car, then always the repentant says that it was complicated it is difficult to find the subject suitable for which they had then resolved to remove me from the mayor with a political manoeuvre, by resigning among the municipal councillor of my majority in context with those of the opposition. And this thing that happened then in November of '94, when I found myself without a majority in the Municipal Councils and therefore with my resignation".

Ruthless ferocity, military capabilities, capillary control of the territory, control of politics, a river of money made with great entrepreneurial ability, but there is another element we have seen that in the history of the Casalesi and of fundamental importance, silence.

Isaia Sales Historian says: "The Casalesi are to the history of the Camorra and like the Corleonesi in the history of the mafia, they have the same importance, except that the Corleonesi are famous, you know everything, many books have been written, the Casalesi have been known and they have only come to the fore in recent years".

For example, the state, the Casalesi mafia has known it for some time. The parliamentary anti-mafia commission arrives in Casal di Principe for the first time in 1990, after the police dissolved a Casalesi Summit at the home of the deputy mayor Corvino and then there are the various investigations and the various trials that have been held over the years, especially the Spartacus trial.

Roberto Saviano, the writer declares: "The incredible thing about Spartacus was first of all the name, for the first time the name of a rebel is given, it is a rather strange process, the rebel was

Spartacus himself, from those lands of the Agro Celano, that is Capua, he revolted, arriving at the Gates of Rome. Spartacus because, because in that land, the law is the real rebellion the real revolt and therefore it was necessary to give the name to those who fought the empire and magistrates give this name, Spartacus to the process that had to fight the empire of the Casalesi clans".

It begins with a repentant, as the Palermo Cosa Nostra maxi-trial started substantially with the declarations of Tommaso Buscetta, the Buscetta of the Casalesi is called Carmine Schiavone is known as Carminuccio and is the cousin of Sandokan. But above all Carminuccio is an entrepreneur, one who knows how to deal with business and public relations specializing in the concrete sector. They arrested him in 1991 and gave him 7 years in prison for some weapons found inside the headquarters of his company. Carminuccio does not stand up and begins to speak with the deputy prosecutors Lucio di Pietro and Federico Cafiero de Raho of the District Anti-

Mafia Directorate of Naples because, in the land of the Casalesi, there is still no DDA. It is also falling in the rest of Campania with the new organized Camorra of Raffaele Cutolo with the new family. Bosses of the calibre of Carmine Alfieri or Pasquale Galasso, they began to talk and with them a river full of repentant. It also happens with the Casalesi who are few, very few, but in any case, there are like Dario De Simone to whom the Casalesi kill their brother-in-law and brother in retaliation, or like Domenico Bidognetti called 'Mimì o` Bruttaccione' the nephew of Cicciotto e` Mezzanotte.

A journalist questions Cicciotto and Mezzanotte who declares: How many people have you killed? Cicciotto replies: "I don't know, 50 or 60 between those I killed and those I had killed. They killed my father because I ... because I can, and I'm revealing so many things, I don't know what it can do, my forgiveness, I give it to you ... Throw in the towel ... You too go to the side of the state, the side of the legality, to be a collaborator you need immense courage, while to be a mafioso you don't need courage".

A pool is born, which also includes substitutes, also substitute prosecutors, Carlo Visconti and Francesco Greco and then Francesco Curcio, Raffaele Falcone and Raffaele Cantone. On December 5, 1995, 3,000 men of the police force raided the Casalesi territory with a list of a hundred people to arrest, they found only 50, some of whom told them they were waiting for them, among the 68 fugitives who did not there is Francesco Schiavone known as Sandokan. Francesco Schiavone arrested him three years later in 1998. He was standing motionless in a secret hiding place in his villa, via Salerno in Casal di Principe, behind a granite wall that moves on a track, together with his wife, his cousin and two daughters. The men of the capturing section have kept an eye on the area, they also pretended to be workers who work the sewers, they even paid you the protection money to look more credible. So, they bet the house, but when they broke, they did not find anyone, then a notice of Carabinieri officer strange in the mouth of ventilation, do you shoot tear gas inside and a voice Sandokan. Don't shoot, my daughters are there, and he gives up. So, there is also him, when after more than ten years from the beginning of the investigations, after 626 hearings that have seen 125 defendants and hundreds of witnesses, the sentence arrives.

Raffaele Magi Councillor declares: "Do you think that we have heard more than 500 witnesses, with examination and cross-examination by the Public Prosecutor and the defence lawyers we have heard more than 20 collaborators of justice, we have acquired more than 100 files of documents relating to wiretapping, in the sentences of other trials starting with the old trials of the Camorra Cutoliana, on which the parties had to speak to limit ourselves to this phase, began in 1998, had a development of about 700 trial hearings, and ended precisely in September 2005".

On September 15, 2005, after an 11-day council chamber, the president of the Court of Assizes of Santa Maria Capua Vetere, reads the sentence. 95 convictions for Camorra association with 21 life sentences, 844 years in prison and over 413 million euros seized. The whole history of the mafia in the province of Caserta, in the 3200 pages of the reasons for the sentence written by judge Raffaele Magi, plus all the other investigations and all the other trials that take place over the years such as Spartacus 2, the police headquarters on relations between the Casalesi politics and finance.

Isaia Sales says: "Towards Spartacus in importance, for the involvement of repentant, for indicted persons, for the number of hearings, for the number of witnesses, for the defence pleadings, it is superior to the Palermo maxi-trial, also for the number of, not only the accused and then condemned".

What should be one of the trials of the century goes by in deafening silence, few articles are very short on the national pages, 50 lines in the daily newspaper Il Mattino di Napoli signed by Rosaria Capacchione, and the rest in the local pages that are read by local readers. and they never get much further. For the rest of Italy, the Casalesi mafia is only a kind of Camorra that is noticed only when it shoots and kills in the streets as after the death of Antonio Bardellino or when a fugitive known as Sandokan is arrested, then everything goes back to oblivion, this always happens when we talk about the mafia in Italy, but a normal crime event is confused with a criminal event and then at that point other crimes are preferred, other more mysterious and more yellow murders.

Rosaria Capacchione declares: "As if you wanted to put a stone on the way of behaving that you have heavily mortgaged, southern Italy is not in the province of Caserta and they do not want to hear about it, because after all if we have a strong organized crime that is not it kills you can also live with it, I don't think so, where and as the patrimonial investigations have shown, all these years that this type of crime especially someone shoots and therefore it is more insidious because it is underground, it ends up taking away any hope of the future to the young people who live in these areas, because it takes away jobs, takes away job prospects, contaminates the market".

Silence is golden, as Gigi Di Fiore writes in a beautiful book called the empire that tells the story of the Casale 'Silence is golden, and reporters, even good informed on time like Rosaria Capacchione or as Sergio Nazzaro who writes mainly on the blog on online magazine had not yet managed to scratch it. Then something happens, a writer arrives and a book arrives Gomorra. The book is called Gomorra and came out in 2006. The circulation of 800 thousand copies which is what a publishing house usually does, when it wants to try with the author it considers promising, runs out in a week.

Roberto Saviano, the writer of the book Gomorra, declares: "The publisher is amazed, who reprints, and I am amazed at myself, and word of mouth leads to a series of positive reviews on all the most important Italian regions. I am invited on television, something changes immediately, after two days of my first television appearance, the book goes on the charts, since then it will never go away, and it happens that I am invited everywhere, the theme slowly starts to leak, hear many books often real masterpieces have been written on the Camorra, essays and also an interesting narrative book that I owe a lot to that Joe Marrazzo's Camorrista, a beautiful book by Nanni Balestrini, Sandokan, had also been written. These books had never reached the general public, and above all, they have always been like little cultists in the work. I'm not telling Casal di Principe or Scampia to the world, but the ambition was to tell the world through the sharing of Scampia, to create a method that would allow us to understand how the criminal economy became the winning economy, this intrigues a lot, enormous Word of mouth, the possibility of understanding certain things".

Gomorra also speaks of the Casalesi, but he does it as a writer's book does, because Saviano is an attentive observer of reality, the names, the figures, the data he writes about are true, but his way of telling, that of a narrator who knows how to do it, because words, images and facts arouse emotions, which is what a writer does nothing more.

Roberto Saviano continues: "When it reached one hundred thousand copies, I feel that my perception of the territory is changing, this exponential growth of readers, of information on the internet of international attention, I don't realize that it would have changed my life. The book becomes a symbol. That's why it becomes a sort of meta book, something special also happens, some bars expose it on the cash desk, as if it were a kind of drawing, cutting out you can say, we are not like our neighbours in the Camorra, but they are quite exposing those for whom the book becomes a symbol and the stories told become stories that belong to a territory, but of which in reality no one has ever really paused to know and read it".

Then another thing happens, it happens that at the end of September 2006 there is an Anti-Mafia demonstration in Casal di Principe, there is a large stage on the market square which is the main square of the town and there are many authorities, c 'is the president of the Chamber Fausto Bertinotti, there is the vice-president of the anti-mafia commission Beppe Lumia, there are local politicians, there are the representatives of the anti-mafia association as free, and there is also him, Roberto Saviano the writer of Gomorra, it's up to him to talk, Roberto Saviano sees all those people, he sees all those guys who look at him, he is from there, he knows what life is like in Casal di Principe, and then what happens to the writers happens to him when they feel something inside who cannot help but say to tell and so he speaks.

Roberto Saviano declares: Then at a certain point I say, Zagaria and Schiavone are worth nothing, go, this land does not belong to you. I remember that something has changed there, because the escort present at the room, when I get up that I am about to leave alone, to take the train, says the boy without our escort does not leave here, and therefore they accompany me to Naples. I leave Naples and go to Pordenone, a literary festival, on which day something happens, so I will return to Pordenone and I will never be a free man again".

It had never happened in Italy that a writer had to be protected by an escort, it had happened abroad, it happened to Salman Rushdie for example, sentenced to death by Ayatollah Khomeini for his satanic verses, it happens in countries dominated by dictatorship, but that is how it is part of Italy dominated by the armed dictatorship of organized crime. While Saviano speaks, Casal di Principe is a cousin of Sandokan who goes around to note those who applaud.

Roberto Saviano: "I end up under guard as I said on October 13, Friday 2006, complicated things happen and anyone who ends up under guard in a marked life but a magistrate for example of the anti-mafia knows that when he was assigned to the DDA (District Anti-Mafia Directorate) will have 7 years of a complicated life, after 7 years he can decide to go back to doing another type of job in the judiciary or Andrea direction of the Antimafia action. In short, he has the time to understand what is happening to him, the day before I was in Pordenone, they call me, to catch a train, and they tell me, Roberto, the prefect said you must have an escort, and I laugh, and already an escort, but that I have become a politician that I need the escort? And on the other side this friend of mine Carabiniere Ciro, with a serious voice saying, Roberto, you need an escort, I'm on the train and I'll see you at the station, he says a patrol will come to take you to the command and I didn't know how to warn my family, the worry let's say more complicated it called a carabiniere who brought me to eat, some carabinieri saw me very tense and they were delightful and try to comfort, 'But don't be afraid of such a thing ', that is, I remember a colonel who came into this room where I was put did, Don't worry, he closed and went back every quarter of an hour, he came greeted me and said again don't worry Everything is fine. I didn't know what was going on. I only know that after a few days I returned to my mother's house with an escort".

It happened that in the meantime after Roberto had spoken to Casal di Principe, there was a report of a justice collaborator who had heard some speeches in prison, some people, bad people, she wondered if Saviano was protected or not. , evaluating whether it was the case not to kill him and at that point, the magistrates who deal with certain things had evaluated for their part whether it was the case to protect Roberto Saviano. There had already been other signs even before and also the way of reporting the news by the local press, certain details, certain particular had seemed a bad signal.

Roberto Saviano says: "Since then everything has changed, they take me to Rome, they take me to houses that are generally houses of witnesses of justice to the repentant. What I remember of these houses, where among other things I live there, which inside the walls preserve the suffering of the people there are, never go out, houses where the water mattress is located, incredible stereo system, flat-screen televisions, because they are houses where you have to try to make the cloister come to life and therefore everyone tries with the money they have as many or as little as they have to improve those 50 square meters, then I also go to houses that I have chosen by myself and authorized by the carabinieri, and for 3 years we start to pay, because unfortunately instead of improving the situation, it gets worse".

The second thing that happens is that an anonymous letter arrives at the editorial office of the espresso, which the carabinieri verify by claiming to be reliable and making it the subject of an information notice, in this anonymous letter someone speaks of a meeting held in a Bisca, where the representatives of the Casalesi families when they have to discuss something. Among the topics under discussion is the project to kill two people, the deputy prosecutor Raffaele Cantone and the writer Roberto Saviano, the leader's vote, no murders, otherwise who knows what happens, the tanks arrive in Casal di Principe, Saviano we do it Holy, no homicide, at least for now. But some vote yes according to the letter and according to the anonymous they would be Nicola Schiavone son of Sandokan and Alessandro Cirillo known as Sergeant, big shots, people who matter, that's why the magistrates say, the anonymous you wrote the letter, because he is afraid that given the calibre of the voters, the decision will be reversed that the murders do the same and since he should be the killer and has no desire to do them and end up in life imprisonment and not being able to Refuse himself, he writes the letter to blow up the operation.

Roberto Saviano declares: "This anonymous worries very much those who defend, who are the carabinieri who manage my security and thus increase my escort, I receive an armoured car and three people".

On March 13, 2008, an appeal hearing is being held in the Spartacus trial, the lawyer Michele Santonastaso is the defender of two Casalesi, Francesco Bidognetti who is in prison and Antonio Iovine who is a fugitive, the lawyer Santonastaso reads a signed letter from both of his clients, a letter of more than 60 pages in which in addition to the law concerning other judicial requests, there is a precise indictment against some people, if they are convicted they write, the fault will be of the substitute Raffaele Cantone's prosecutor of the writer's deputy prosecutor Federico Cafiero de Raho so write with hatred with contempt Roberto Saviano and the morning chronicler Rosaria Capacchione.

Rosaria Capacchione declares: "This document read in an anomalous way because you do not read those documents are generally deposited, thinking of imputation, it is read by the Anti-Mafia prosecutor, as an explicit threat to the persons named, as if these people had been indicated at all 'external so that no measures were taken, so it is read after a few days we were in the middle of March a few days before Easter, I have the supply for the first time, and since then life has changed a bit".

Life changes, Roberto Saviano knows it and Rosaria Capacchione knows that she is a journalist and should go around unnoticed, listen, talk to people who may not want to be noticed, and how do you do it with two carabinieri or two policemen always behind you, no, life changes when you are under guard and maybe you didn't count it in your job.

Rosaria Capacchione says: "That day when I was told that I would have an escort, I was on the street I was going to work at the newspaper, on foot, I was told that there was a car waiting for me, I had to report where I was in that moment, I cheated a bit, I took an hour to take a walk, the last one alone, then I had since that day, a few days before Easter, always two men with me who accompany me for a long time and now it still happens to me to dream of escaping, using a secondary gate, of my park to go away, because it is not so much the presence but the idea of presence and the idea of the lack of freedom in suddenly deciding to do something, this morning I had to go out at 7, I couldn't have done it, I had to call, warn, get someone to come, suddenly things can't be done anymore".

Escort at the highest level for the two magistrates, escort for Rosaria Capacchione and reinforced escort for Roberto Saviano, who in the meantime had another sign of the danger of his situation. It comes from the Anti-Mafia investigative department of Milan that has had information on the project to kill Roberto Saviano by Christmas, we make you this panettone someone would have said, confirmation is requested from a collaborator of justice, Carmine Schiavone, who denies knowing anything about the Christmas project, which, however, confirms that there is a death sentence for Roberto Saviano.

Roberto Saviano declares: "Every six months, the Casalesi family made known a man sentenced to death, even the writings are very important, a coffin is drawn, Il Mattino in these photos, on the house of Carmine Schiavone it is no coincidence, a house uninhabited by a decade, this coffin appears with my name written on it, then the usual writings, Saviano shit, Saviano toxic, because those written are important because in Casal di Principe they were never written on the walls, some writing was sports, but a country that has always maintained a custom in this sense, very rich things, a strict country, then it was also forbidden to take drugs, but first they gave the authorization to make joints near the cemetery, but the rigour is total".

Another thing also happens, it always happens, in bad faith or even in good faith or simply for lack of information, it is the barrage of doubts that inevitably affects anyone who has to do with certain things, even if they are on the other side. part of the state, of the law and the people, it also happens to Roberto Saviano, one wonders if his story is not just a hoax if he really takes risks or is not simply playing the hero. Basically, he is not a magistrate or an investigator, and he is not even a politician, he is only a writer. It will not be an invention of the publishing house? A hype to sell more copies? Because I have sold several copies of Saviano's book, we are already at 2 million.

Saviano says: "What I have earned is much less than any area leader of the Casalesi clan can earn. But no one in the territory I come from has ever dared to mention the earnings of criminal organizations, earnings often made from toxic waste with the earnings that have soared, the number of cancer deaths and deformed defects, according to the magazine, the largest. oncology magazine, no one has ever made a demonstration, a declaration, I speak of my villagers and not of the construction companies, against these types of characters, they got rich on the trafficking of toxic waste, they did it very well".

For example, there is an actor from Lodi called Giulio Cavalli, he brought some shows against the mafia to the theatre, he made names and surnames, and now he too, like Roberto Saviano and under guard, and they say the same about him too. exaggerating, play the hero. But be careful, because here we are not talking about poses and attitudes, we are talking about a state service, the escort, which must be approved by the ministry, and which is not given like this for nothing, especially the actors and especially the writers. Bertolt Brecht said Blessed is that country that does not need heroes, Italy is not that blessed country, heroes are useful to us and how, they are especially useful in times of war and against organized crime, against the Camorra and also against the Casalesi mafia is a war.

If the first sentence of the Spartacus trial had practically not appeared in the press after the spotlight turned on by Saviano, and on Saviano, but no matter why the spotlights are needed, the second sentence, that of appeal, on June 18, 2008, is full of sent from all over the world. After the trial of the Spartacus appeal trial, he called to judge years of ferocious crimes of the Camorra linked to the Casalesi clan, the sentence was expected after three days, meanwhile, The Godfather Francesco Schiavone has returned to make his voice heard. The sentence largely confirms the previous one, life imprisonment for the leaders of the Casalesi in prisons such as Francesco Schiavone, Francesco Bidognetti, and life imprisonment for the leaders of the Casalesi fugitives such as Antonio Iovine and Michele Zagaria. The cassation sentence is still missing but, in the meantime, it is a battle that has been won both from a judicial and information point of view. But be careful, it is only a battle the war continues, because in the meantime the spring campaign begins. There is a man named Giuseppe Setola who is part of the clan of Francesco Bidognetti, they call him 'o` Cecato', that is the blind man because he has a problem with one eye it is for this reason that despite a conviction in the first degree to life imprisonment for murder, is under house arrest in Pavia. But the problem must not be so serious because when Giuseppe Setola shoots, he sees very well and in any case in April 2008 he escapes from house arrest. As a fugitive, Giuseppe Setola leads a firing group with a very specific strategy.

Luigi Di Fiore, Journalist and Writer declare: "He managed to gather 30 very fierce and bloodthirsty people who followed him in this whole strategy that had precise criminal objectives, one to eliminate and cut the ground under the feet of the repentant, therefore through their family members, two dates of the warnings to the entrepreneurs who denounced, there was, therefore, the murder of Noviello, the murder of Granata, give a warning to all groups of Africans who deal in drugs in the area, exploit prostitution that historically paid the bribe to the Casalesi to make these activities more visible, more dangerous in the area and therefore increase the price of the bribe to Africans".

The first to fall under the blows of the men of the district on May 2, 2008, is Umberto Bidognetti, his father Domenico, grandson of Cicciotto and Mezzanotte who had repented, they kill him in his buffalo farm firing at him more than 12 shots plus the one of grace, ahead. On May 16, 2008, the Casalesi di Setola killed Domenico Noviello. Domenico Noviello is a 65-year-old man, a respectable man, who 7 years earlier had said 'No' no to the tax collectors of Cicciotto and midnight who asked him for protection money for his driving school in Castelvolturno, had had him arrested, had remained under guard until 2008 and then judged that there was no longer any danger that they had removed it. On May 16, Mr Noviello is in his car and is going to have a coffee before going to the driving school as he does every morning. When you see some people approaching, immediately imagine what's going to happen and try to get out of the car, but can't. 20 gunshots, the last one is the final blow to him too, to the head. On 2 June 2008, instead, Michele Orsi was killed, he was shot on the first step of the bar he is entering in Casal di Principe. Michele Orsi was a fairly controversial waste disposal consortium director, he had been involved in an investigation and had started talking to the magistrates who were given many names, names of politicians and Camorra, when they shoot him, he is alone, without they have never assigned him any escort. 11 July 2008 they kill Raffaele Granata, who has a bathing establishment in Marina di Varcaturo. Mr Raphael is the case of the bar when they arrive two boys with a bike, take the helmets even when they come down from the bike and this is a bad sign, pointing straight up to the bar and fire at him 10 shots calibre 9.

There are many people that Giuseppe Setola who kills in the spring campaign, commits 18 murders in the space of 5 months, among these episodes there is also a massacre, on the evening of September 18, after killing a man in Baia Verde, a relative of an affiliate, a man who had somehow given some news to the investigators, a third or fourth level figure in the criminal landscape, but functional to the interests of the clan. They had already tried before in August around 7 in the evening, they had passed with two motorcycles and a van in front of the headquarters of the Nigerian Association of Campania, Bristle had leaned on the grating of the gate with a Kalashnikov, two others had entered the courtyard and they had fired with two guns, 6 people perish but the whole head and chest, which means they shot to kill. On September 18, 2008, they try again around 9:30 in the evening, the car with Giuseppe Setola and his Killers on board stops in front of a tailor shop run by African immigrants in Castel Volturno, Setola gets off with an automatic pistol and begins to shoot people outside the club while two other killers descend with a machine gun in Kalashnikov and unload them inside the tailor's shop, kill 6 people and injure another.

Saviano says: "A massacre, which in the following days provokes the protest of the African community. After that massacre, the Africans take to the streets, stop an entire city and say never again, never dare again. The thought that came to me when I saw this revolt was that the Africans did not come only to do jobs that the Italians no longer want to do, but they also came to defend the rights that the Italians no longer want to defend and the revolt against the clan was a mass revolt of the African community, women, children, never seen. They shouted, "We come here to this land to work and live, do not dare to take away that we have sacrificed everything", and it is interesting to remember that the only two revolts made in Italy in the last 20 years against the mafia were Castel Volturno from African communities and Rosarno for a similar episode that the 'Ndrangheta killed a person, an African and Rosarno in Calabria to which he says about the revolt against the African community against the 'Ndrangheta".

In addition to the African immigrants who come to work in one way or another, there is also a crime of course it is with that, especially Nigerian crime, the Casalesi had already agreed, shooting. In 1990 they had killed 5 people and injured another 7 by shooting at a bar frequented by Africans in Mondragone. They had contracted out the Nigerian bad luck, drug dealing, black prostitution and even the market for the exploitation of illegal immigrants in gruelling jobs such as picking tomatoes and in return they took a big bribe. But on September 18, 2008, Bristle and his team shot in the pile hitting people of different nationalities and who had nothing to do with drug dealing with crime, so much so that the judiciary attributes the massacre to the aggravating circumstance of terrorism, massacre and terrorism, this is Giuseppe Setola's spring campaign.

Federico Cafiero of the Public Prosecutor declares: "These very serious events were all followed with a single purpose, that of fully regaining control of the territory, it was necessary to recover credibility in the eyes of the population of Caserta and not only of Caserta, someone had started to refuse payment, someone else had made accusatory statements against them, but the Spartacus sentence had also been a big blow to the organization because it had sanctioned the life-long detention of historical leaders for the organization, all this had determined the resolution of the strategy which, as I said, was a massacre strategy".

Giuseppe Setola is not a bloodthirsty killer, he is not even a crazy splinter, he is an executor who puts in place a planned and organized strategy, then at the beginning of 2009 the carabinieri identify his hiding place. Giuseppe Setola is not the only Casalesi fugitive to end up in handcuffs in recent times, it is not only the men who end up in the hands of the law but also the money. In July 2009, real estate, land, seized from the Clan of Francesco Bidognetti, which is that of Giuseppe Setola companies, shops, bars and even trucks and tankers were, for a total value of 50 million euros.

Saviano declares: "It seems that Casalesi is arrested every day and that the clan loses money in the maxi kidnappings every day, but we are still far from Vittoria unfortunately, it is first of all just think that most of the kidnappings are coming against a single clan, that the Bidognetti clan, therefore a single clan of the corporation that has been disrupted, there are also other families still very powerful, there are two fugitives Michele Zagaria and Antonio Iovine, it is they who must be stopped because they are the ones who do business with cement, they are the ones who do business in the investment".

Despite the convictions in the trials, despite the arrests and kidnappings, the Casalesi, the car of the province of Caserta, are still there, indeed, they have never left, they control the territory with the same capillarity, with the same brazen demonstration of power, in the local press, for example, letters from Boss fugitives or restricted to 41 bis appear like Francesco Schiavone who send messages to the affiliates, clarify internal problems or report targets to be hit, or direct phone calls arrive from fugitive Bosses such as Michele Zagaria and Antonio Iovine who dictates do not deny and claim to influence the articles.

A direct phone call from Bosses Michele Zagaria and Antonio Iovine: Michele Zagaria exclaims: "Listen, I'm Michele Zagaria, then listen to me carefully, I'm calling you because I want to say, right, that you are not a serious journalist." the journalist exclaims on the phone: "Yes, Excuse me for a moment, you are Michele Zagaria Who?". Michele Zagaria replies: "you know who writes it in the newspaper, right? Who is at war with Antonio Iovine"? The journalist replies: "But is ... excuse me is this a joke?" Michele Zagaria replies:

"No, no, no, it's not a joke, it's me personally, that's how I do things to you because I'm a serious person and you are not ... Wait a minute, I'll pass you Antonio Iovine too, okay, so you take away this thought of always writing bullshit, bullshit ... I think you ware a serious professional, right? You don't write all this bullshit., Of course, now I'll pass him on to you. " Antonio Iovine goes on the phone exclaiming: "Hello, I'm Antonio Iovine… Look, we're not kidding because we got tired of doing all this stupid, right? We are families that we have respected for many years, so if you have to write news, write them seriously and write the truth. " The reporter exclaims: "May I know something? Where are you calling from?" Iovine replies: "Us…? From America, is it important, is this important…?" the journalist replies: "It is essential" Iovine replies: "Eh, but for what reason?" the journalist replies: "I need proof to know that it is you" Michele Zagaria replies in a harsh voice: "Listen to me, then tomorrow I'll send you my brother with the document and

Antonio's brother with the document, and you see that they go together and all this problem has cleared up, it's clear, isn't it? Enough ... we are not threatening you, and nothing, okay? " The journalist exclaims: "Okay" and Michele adds: "Do you want confirmation that I am sending you my brother? Or can this be enough? " The journalist exclaims: "Yes is enough for me." Michele adds: "Why you asked, don't you know that I'm a fugitive?".

The Casalesi are indeed there and continue to cultivate a close relationship with politics that is more of a partisan relationship than a mafia in a Camorra clan, with whoever is enough to be in power.

Raffaele Cantone Magistrate says: "It is no coincidence that even recently the city council was dissolved for infiltrations involving the Casalesi clan, it is no coincidence that in recent investigations it has been verified, for example, how the Zagaria group was in charge of managing the municipal elections of their country, was in the wiretaps, the followers of the clan talked about the lessons of my little horse to indicate the subjects who were somehow sponsored by the clan".

In the investigations of the DDA, politicians of the national level end up like Undersecretary Nicola Cosentino, accused of being in the hands of Francesco Bidognetti for justice collaborators such as Dario De Simone and Gaetano Vassallo those of waste. But be careful, accusations and investigations are still being examined by the judiciary, Undersecretary Cosentino denies having ever had anything to do with organized crime. The Casalesi are there and continue to make money, a lot of money, since only the seizures of liquid assets that took place in 2008 by the law, amounted to 400 million euros, it is a company that can cope without problems, losses of these entities, it is certainly a very rich society, so rich that it reaches abroad, as confirmed by the investigations of the deputy prosecutor Raffaele Cantone and other magistrates who reach as far as Scotland or Germany, where, unlike the 'Ndrangheta, the Casalesi do not have killed anyone and therefore they are not known, but above all in Eastern Europe, in Poland, in Romania where they bought companies, estates, properties.

Rosaria Capacchione declares: "In those parts, it is even more difficult to intervene from a judicial point of view because not all those countries have bilateral treaties that allow extradition or recognition of the crime of crime and mafia association".

Moreover, that it was not a problem linked to the south of Campania, in particular, was clear to everyone for a long time. For example, there is the financial mind of the Zagaria clan, Pasquale Zagaria known as 'Bin Laden', who thanks to an entrepreneur from Parma gets to buy a building from Parma to the centre of Milan, there is Raffaele Diana called 'Rafilotto', the Man from Sandokan in the province of Modena recently arrested, his men manage premises in Carpi and

Castelfranco Emilia, get their hands on the contracts in the area, they also ask entrepreneurs for protection money even from inside the Modena prison in which they are locked up, in May 2007 Giuseppe Pagano was shot in the leg, an entrepreneur who does not pay and indeed denounces his construction site in Riolo near Castelfranco Emilia. The Casalesi do business in the north in the rest of Italy and abroad, but we must always remember that they are not entrepreneurs but criminals, their easy money pollutes the legal economy by poisoning it like a virus, and the methods always remain the same, the control of the territory in the land dominated by the armed dictatorship of the Casalesi does not mean development, but death. Michele Landa is a night watchman from Mondragone, a security guard who has the task of monitoring a telephone repeater in Pescopagano, it is not a good job, the area is a bad area of the crime of peddling, and that repeater had already suffered an attack when he was in Aversa in 2005, they had killed another security guard Nicola San Marco, Michele Landa is standing there in front of the repeater in his car alone and he is afraid, but I have only 2 months left to retire and then he can return to the countryside in the piece of land he works every day to supplement his salary.

Angelina Landa daughter of Michele Landa declares:

On September 6, 2006, when my father had to return at 6 am from the night shift, my mother at around 7:30 begins to worry as she does not come back, she calls me immediately and I try to reassure her she will surely stay at the bar, don't worry, in the meantime I try to call him on his cell phone, but he didn't answer or was off. In the summer we are all immediately on the move, the first thing I did I called the Central in Caserta and where they told me that they had no news, now they would be informed. "

Michele Landa died, killed in his car which was taken away, set on fire and thrown into a ditch in the Mondragone countryside, where he is found 4 days later, Michele Landa's family members receive his remains one piece at a time by hand. that searches are made in the car and they have to be taken away in a shoebox.

Angelina Landa declares: "We find ourselves on September 27 with many people who are close to us and show us their pain, it was for the good they wanted my father, but there was not even an institutional figure presenting the institution and here my idea goes to force that we live in a place where there is no state. "

Because Michele Landa is a lot, because too many economic interests revolved around that repeater or because they wanted to make it a return horse, steal it and ask for the ransom for its return. In any case, Michele Lando died because this is how we live we die in the lands dominated by the armed dictatorship of the mafia.

Angelina declares: "I am pleased to tell the story of my father, to show all people, as respectable as us, how easy it is to be involved in the Camorra in a land where there is no right, this is the message

I want to send to all the people of my land, where living with it is not just looking from the outside as a spectator, but sooner or later you find yourself involved and then you have to justify others because it happened to your father. "

The Casalesi in the sense of the Camorra of Casal di Principe and surroundings are there, but there are also the other Casalesi, in the sense of the people who live in Casal di Principe and surroundings and are not criminals, indeed, they are not even indifferent but give themselves to do to restore a clean meaning to that word Casalesi. There are individuals and there are associations, such as Libera or the Don Peppino Diana association, cultural initiatives but also concrete things such as the recovery of assets confiscated from the Casalesi, the bad ones, to return them to the good ones through management for the community.

Giuseppe Pagano, Member of the Cooperative 'Nuova Cucina Organizzata' declares: "We called the Restaurant NCO Nuova Cucina Organizzata.

We start from an assumption, this land is made up of people where there are no problems of sociability, of being together, of dialogue, of sharing difficulties, then we go to recover what are the things of our territory, the things positive, so we focus on this".

It is not an easy task, because the struggle here is not only against the military domination of the territory but against a habit, a mentality, a series of values that make the rich Camorrista an example to imitate and a model to achieve.

There is another Enemy to fight and that is indifference, but the indifference of those who are far away, of those who live elsewhere and who think that everything that happens over there in Casal di Principe and its surroundings, in the dominated lands by the armed dictatorship of the Camorra, all in all, it does not concern him, that he died more, one mayor more threatened, one more arrest, one more seizure of assets, all in all, it does not make the news. Here ends our story, the one we are telling us, because the story of the

Casalesi, of the mafia in the province of Caserta, is not over yet. It's not over for Lorenzo Diana who has been living under guard for 14 years, since the Casalesi sentenced him to death for his political activity, it is not over for Renato Natale, former mayor of Casal di Principe, who does not have an escort. because he denounced us, to continue to do his job as a doctor among immigrants, it is not over for Rosaria Capacchione and Roberto Saviano who must stay under guard for fear of being killed, and it did not end of course for all Respectable Casalesi living under the armed dictatorship of the Camorra.

Dario De Simone repentant and collaborator of justice declares: "I tell the new generations who are in those areas, in my villages and nearby, not to look at these people with admiration, no ... They are dogs like I was a dog, and these are They have no courage, there is no respect, there is nothing and for no one, neither for the territory nor for the people nor the neighbour, they have no respect even for their families, for their wives, it is not power, the person of respect is no longer afraid. "

But perhaps there would be a way to end this story, it would be to not leave those people alone to be heroes, a country that does not need heroes and also a country where heroes are all sincerely and naturally, where everyone and not. only a few, they come out to say, Iovine, Zagaria, Schiavone, but also Riina, Messina Denaro and the gentlemen of the Ndrangheta, corrupt politicians, unfaithful officials and unscrupulous entrepreneurs, who poison the earth, the economy and the soul of the people. here, tells everyone you are nothing, you are worth nothing, go away, this land is not yours.

About the Author

M. Esposito (1972) Southend on sea East London
Book Pubblished:
- Men calls ego –
- Uomo Chiama Ego –
- Mafia Camorra and Casal di Principe

Education: Fallen in via Fani Napoli (1976)
- Work carried out:
- Casiltex
- London Club International
- William Hill
- Business partnership London
- Le Follie

Notes

Notes

Printed in Great Britain
by Amazon